MALORIE BLACKMAN

Girl Wonder's Winter Adventures

Illustrated by Lis Toft

PUFFIN BOOKS

PUFFIN BOOKS

Published by the Penguin Group
Penguin Books Ltd, 27 Wrights Lane, London W8 5 TZ, England
Penguin Books USA Inc., 375 Hudson Street, New York, New York 10014, USA
Penguin Books Australia Ltd, Ringwood, Victoria, Australia
Penguin Books Canada Ltd, 10 Alcorn Avenue, Toronto, Ontario, Canada M4V 3B2
Penguin Books (NZ) Ltd, 182–190 Wairau Road, Auckland 10, New Zealand

Penguin Books Ltd, Registered Offices: Harmondsworth, Middlesex, England

First published by Victor Gollancz Ltd 1992
Published in Puffin Books 1994
1 3 5 7 9 10 8 6 4 2

Filmset by Datix International Limited, Bungay, Suffolk
Printed in England by Clays Ltd, St Ives plc
Set in 15/18 pt Monophoto Garamond

To Neil
with love and affection,
and to the best mum
in the world
M.B.

Contents

Blackberry Gravy, Blackberry Soup!

Hooray! Today we're going blackberry picking. Mum says that "winter is just beginning, when blackberries need picking".

"Now then, Maxine and Antony and Edward, I want you three on your best behaviour," Mum said as we set off in the car.

As if we're ever on anything else!

We drove to some woods near to where we live. The woods were filled with blackberry bushes with heaps and Loads and TONS of blackberries on them. There were lots of other people there as well. We got out of our car and looked around.

Then I had a brilliant idea.

I turned to my brothers and said, "Antony and Edward, we're going to pick more blackberries than anyone else here. In fact we're going to pick more blackberries than everyone else put together."

"How are we going to do that?" Antony asked.

"Yeah, how?" Edward said.

So I replied, "I think this is a job for Girl Wonder . . ."

"And the Terrific Twins. Yippee!" the twins shouted.

And we spun around until we were galloping giddy.

"OK, Terrific Twins," I said. "We're going to pick blackberries and not stop until we've got tons and tons."

Mum gave each of us a big wicker basket. We all walked over to one of the mega-tall blackberry bushes and found a space. Then we picked blackberries off the

bush and put them into our baskets. We picked and plucked and pulled and we didn't stop. In fact, the twins and I carried on after everyone else had stopped for a rest.

"Come on you three. You needn't work so hard. Let's stop for lunch," Mum said.

"We can't stop. We're going to pick more blackberries than anyone else," I replied.

"But I'm hungry," Anthony moaned.

"But I'm starving," Edward groaned.

"Come on Terrific Twins," I whispered so Mum wouldn't hear. "We're super heroes. We have to pick more blackberries than anyone else."

"Oh, all right then," grumbled Antony.

"Oh, OK then," mumbled Edward.

Sometimes being a super hero is hard work!

So we carried on plucking and pulling and picking the blackberries whilst Mum ate some lunch. After her lunch Mum came back and started working again, but at least we hadn't stopped. It was getting quite late when the twins started to complain.

"My arms ache," muttered Antony.

"My . . . my hands hurt," spluttered Edward.

My whole body was hurting by now.

"OK, Terrific Twins. I think that's enough for today. Our baskets are tip-top full," I said.

Including Mum's basket we had four baskets overflowing with blackberries.

It was wonderful.

Mum looked a bit worried though.

"I didn't expect you to pick so many blackberries. What am I going to do with them all?" Mum said.

When we got home, we carried the baskets of blackberries into the kitchen.

"We did a great job, Terrific Twins," I said.

"A mega-wonderful job," agreed Antony.

"A mega-wonderful, brilliant job," said Edward.

We had chicken and rice for dinner, followed by blackberries and they were mega-delicious and we still had whole basketfuls left.

The next morning when we went down for breakfast, I was starving. I knew why too. My brothers and I had had no lunch the previous day. I decided to eat huge amounts to make up for it.

"What's for breakfast, Mum?" I asked.

"Toast and some blackberry jam I made last night from the blackberries you picked," Mum replied.

The blackberry jam was scrumptious. And Mum had mushed and crushed some blackberries and added milk to them to make a lovely yoghurty drink.

The twins and I played in the garden until lunch time.

"What's for lunch, Mum?" we asked when we got hungry.

"Sausages, mashed potatoes and blackberry gravy followed by an apple and blackberry pie and a milk and blackberry drink," Mum replied.

Blackberry gravy?

"Antony, what do you think of the blackberry gravy?" I asked as we started to eat.

"It's not too bad," he sniffed.

"It's not too good either," Edward said, whiffing it.

"Hhmm!" I said.

Then came tea-time. And what did we have? Blackberry soup to start, followed by fish and blackberries instead of peas and our pudding was ice-cream and blackberries. And with our meal we had more mashed, crushed, scrushed blackberries which Mum strained into a jug to make blackberry juice.

"Mum, not more blackberries," I said, dismayed when I saw our tea.

"Yeah, not more blackberries," Antony agreed.

"Oh no! Not more blackberries," said Edward.

We'd all had enough of blackberries for a while.

"I'm not letting good blackberries go to waste and I'm not going to let them spoil and rot in their baskets either," Mum said, her hands on her hips. "So we'll carry on eating the blackberries until they're all finished."

"All four baskets?" we asked.

"ALL four baskets," Mum replied.

Yuk!

Mum went into the kitchen to get some more blackberry juice.

"See what you've done, Maxine," Antony frowned at me.

"Yeah, we'll be eating rotten blackberries until Christmas," said Edward.

"My plan worked though," I replied. "We did pick more blackberries than anyone else."

"So what?" Antony said. "Your plan was mega-stinky."

"Yeah! Seriously mega-stinky," Edward agreed.

Being a super hero is definitely very hard work!

Extra Special Scary

"Heh! Heh! Heh! Heh!" I cackled.

I was practising being an evil witch for Hallowe'en. We were going to my cousin Jayne's Hallowe'en party.

"You don't look scary at all," Antony said. He was dressed in a ghost costume which was just a sheet with two eye holes cut out of it. "I'm more scary than you. I'm a good ghost. Oooooh! Oooooooooh!"

"I'm the most scary of all," Edward argued.

He was dressed as a Hallowe'en pumpkin.

"What sort of noise does a Hallowe'en

19

pumpkin make?" Edward asked.

I thought for a moment.

"I'm not sure." I frowned. "I'm not sure it makes a noise at all. If it does I expect it's a kind of whee-squiiiish, whee-squiiiish sound."

"Whee-squiiiish! Whee-squiiiish!" Edward said. Then he complained. "That doesn't sound very scary."

Mum came into the kitchen.

"You all look very good." She smiled.

"But do we look scary?" I asked.

"Yeah! Really scary?" said Antony.

"Extra special scary?" asked Edward.

"Er . . . you look . . . very good," Mum replied.

But not scary! Mum must have seen our faces drop.

"The only reason you don't look scary to me is because I made your costumes," Mum said quickly. "None of you could ever be scary to me. Cheer up you three. We're going to Jayne's party soon. I'll just

get Jayne's presents from the living-room and then we'll set off."

'We're not scary," Antony wailed as soon as Mum left the kitchen.

"Not scary at all," howled Edward.

"We could be scary . . ." I began.

"How?" asked Antony.

"Yeah, how?" said Edward.

"I'm not sure," I said. "But I think this is a job for Girl Wonder and . . ."

"The Terrific Twins," said my brothers.

And we all spun around until the kitchen dipped and dived around us.

"Do you have a plan, Girl Wonder?" Antony asked.

"A good plan, please!" Edward added quickly.

I thought and thought. Then I had an ace-wonderful idea. But then my ideas are always ace-wonderful. (Which is why I don't understand why they often get us into a lot of trouble. This one wouldn't though. Mum would like this one!)

"Mum says that we don't frighten her, but if we could make her jump, that would prove that we're super-duper scary. The scariest!" I said.

"So what should we do to make her jump?" Antony asked.

"Drop an ice-cube down her back?" Edward suggested.

"I don't think she'd like that somehow."
I shook my head.

"How about if we drop a worm down her back?" Antony said, excited.

I thought for a moment.

"I don't think she'd like that one either." I sighed.

It was a shame because both the ice-cube and the worm were good ideas.

"How about . . . how about if we got a frog from Miss Ree's pond and drop that down Mum's back?" Antony said.

"That's it!" I said.

"Brilliant!" said Edward.

We all thought that was a wonderful idea. There was just one problem. How could we get into Miss Ree's garden, get the frog and get back home without being seen? Miss Ree is our grumpy next door neighbour and if she saw us in her garden we'd be in big, BIG trouble!

"I know!" I grinned. "We could drop Frodo, my rubber frog, down Mum's back and pretend it's a frog from Miss Ree's pond."

"Will that scare Mum?" Antony asked.

"No, it won't," Edward said.

"Yes it will, if we do it right," I argued. And I told the Terrific Twins my super-duper, ace-wonderful plan.

"Not bad," Antony said, surprised.

"Not *too* bad," agreed Edward.

We all dashed up to my bedroom to get Frodo off my pillow where he slept every night.

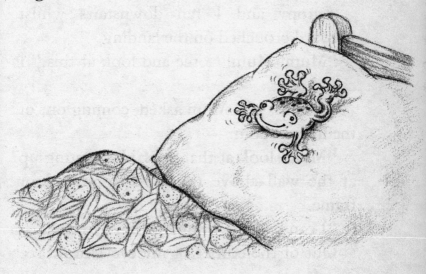

"OK, Terrific Twins," I said. "I'll get Mum to stand in the hall. Edward, you have to creep down the stairs without Mum hearing you. When you're close enough you can drop Frodo down the back of Mum's blouse. Then you, Antony, must make a noise like a mad frog."

"This is going to be fun," laughed Antony.

"Yes it is." Edward clapped his hands.

"This is sure to make Mum say we're the scariest," I said happily.

Antony and I ran downstairs whilst Edward crouched on the landing.

"Mum! Mum! Come and look at this," I called out.

"What is it?" Mum asked, coming out of the living-room.

"Mum, look at that," I said, pointing up at the wall above the living-room's door frame.

"I can't see anything." Mum frowned.

Out of the corner of my eye I could see

Edward tip-toeing down the stairs. But
Mum was too far away from the banisters
for Edward to reach her.

"You'll have to move back a bit to see
it," I said to Mum.

"To see what? What are you talking
about, Maxine?" Mum asked.

"Stand back here against the banisters,
Mum," I said. "Then you'll see it."

Mum took a step backwards to stand against the banisters.

"I still don't see . . ."

I looked up. Edward pulled back the neck of Mum's blouse and dropped my frog Frodo down her back.

"It's a frog from next door's pond," I said quickly.

"Cro-oo-oak! Cro-oo-oak! Rei-ei-bit! Cro-oo-oak!" Antony called out, jumping

up and down and all around just like a frog himself.

Mum screamed and pulled the bottom of her blouse out of her skirt. She screamed again as Frodo hit the carpet and bounced around her. Antony, Edward and I creased up laughing. I laughed so hard that my witch's hat fell off.

"We scared you! We scared you!" we called out.

I picked up my frog. "It's just Frodo," I laughed. "Look Mum, it's just Frodo."

Mum stared at us without saying a word. Then her lips began to twitch, then to quiver, then to quaver. Then she burst out laughing. I don't think she wanted to – it's just that she couldn't help it.

"You three are going to drive me bonkers!" Mum laughed.

"We were going to use a real frog out of Miss Ree's pond," Antony began.

"Yeah! But we decided to use Maxine's frog instead," said Edward.

Mum's smile instantly disappeared. "I'm glad you decided not to drop a *real* frog down my back," she said quietly. "I wouldn't have liked that. I wouldn't have liked that one little bit."

The way Mum said it made me think we'd had a very lucky escape! I don't think Mum would have laughed quite so much if Frodo had been a real frog!

"Come on, you three." Mum smiled. "Time to go to your cousin Jayne's party."

As we walked to the car Antony said, "Your plan to scare Mum wasn't as seriously smelly as your plans usually are."

"Yeah! Not too smelly at all," said Edward.

"I do get it right sometimes." I grinned.

Snow
Please!

As soon as my eyes were open I was awake.
I jumped out of bed and ran to my bedroom
window. I drew back the curtains eagerly
and . . . no snow! Where was the snow? It
was pouring with rain but – NO SNOW!

It wasn't really winter without snow and
snowmen and snowball fights and catching
freezing, falling snow on your tongue and
feeling it melt.

WHERE WAS THE SNOW?

I had my wash and got dressed before
going downstairs. Mum took one look at
my face and said, "What's the matter with
you, Maxine?"

"I want it to snow," I replied.

"I want it to snow too," said Antony.

"And me," agreed Edward.

"Well, there's nothing you, I or anyone else can do about that," Mum said.

"Would you like it to snow, Mum?" I asked.

"Yes I would." Mum smiled. "I love the snow."

Mum went into the kitchen to get our breakfast.

"Antony, Edward, we're going to make it snow," I whispered to my twin brothers.

"How are we going to do that?" Antony asked with a frown.

"Yeah, how?" Edward repeated.

"Er . . . I haven't worked that bit out yet, but this is definitely a job for Girl Wonder . . ."

"And the Terrific Twins," laughed Antony and Edward.

And we all stood up and whirled and twirled around until we almost knocked the table over.

"So what do we do now, Girl Wonder?" asked Antony.

"Yeah, what?" said Edward.

"All three of us will have to think about that one," I replied.

Just then, Mum walked into the living-room with our breakfast, so I couldn't say any more.

"You three are quiet. What are you up to now?" Mum asked suspiciously, as we sat eating our breakfast at the table.

"Mum, why won't it snow?" I asked.

"It's not cold enough yet," Mum said. "When it's cold enough, falling rain turns into snow."

"Oh I see . . ." I said.

"Your dad's grandma used to tell me about the snow they had in Barbados," Mum carried on.

"I thought Barbados was hot?" I said.

"It is. It never gets cold enough there for snow, so at Christmas Grandma's family used to sprinkle marl throughout the house and in the garden. That made it look like it had been snowing everywhere – even inside the house." Mum chuckled. "Of course that was a long time ago."

"What's marl, Mum?" Antony asked.

"Marl is like chalk, little bits of white chalk," Mum explained. "And sprinkled around the house it looks just like snow."

And that's when I had my extra-brilliant idea.

After breakfast, whilst Mum was busy fixing the light in the twins' bedroom, I told my plan to my brothers.

"We'll make it snow in the house, just like Dad's grandma's family used to do in Barbados," I said.

"How will we do that?" Antony asked.

"Yeah, just how?" said Edward.

"That's a good question." I frowned. "We need something white like chalk to sprinkle around."

"How about flour?" Antony suggested.

We all had a think.

"No! Flour is too fine. It'd disappear into the carpet," I decided.

"Then how about sugar?" said Edward.

We all had another think.

"Nah! Sugar is too sticky. Our feet would stick to the carpet," I replied.

"I got it!" I said. "This is super-duper brilliant. We'll sprinkle the washing-powder Mum uses to get our clothes clean all around the house. Washing-powder is white and looks like snow. It'll be a big surprise for Mum."

"That's a good idea, Girl Wonder." Antony nodded.

"Not bad," said Edward.

"It's mega-brilliant!" I argued. "After all, Mum said she'd like some snow."

We went into the conservatory where the washing-machine was kept. Antony and Edward started arguing about who should sprinkle the washing-powder until I said, "There's no need for that. There's plenty of washing-powder for all of us to have a go. Besides, super heroes don't argue."

So Antony sprinkled washing-powder in the conservatory and the kitchen. I did the living-room and Edward used the last of the washing-powder in the hall and at the bottom of the stairs.

And when we'd finished, it looked TERRIFIC!

"Mum, come and see what we did," I called out.

"What is it?" Mum asked, walking down the stairs.

She stopped half-way down the stairs and stared at the hall carpet. It's usually beige but now it was white and looked just like snow on the ground.

"What . . . on . . . earth . . . ?" Mum stared at the carpet. AND STARED AND STARED. Then she finally looked at us. I recognized that look. We were in serious trouble! Again!

"WHAT IS THAT . . . THAT ON MY CARPET?" Mum asked furiously.

"It's snow," I answered.

"That's right. Snow," said Antony.

"Yeah, snow," said Edward.

"Snow! I'll give you snow!" Mum marched down the stairs. "That's my washing-powder all over my good carpets. Right, you three. Out with the vacuum cleaner. NOW."

We spent all morning vacuuming up the washing-powder. The vacuum cleaner couldn't suck up some of it, so we had to get down on our hands and knees and pick up every single grain.

"No more pocket money for any of you until that box of washing-powder is paid for," Mum ranted and raved behind us.

"Maxine, your idea was rotten rubbish," Antony moaned at me.

"Yeah, extra stinky rotten rubbish," groaned Edward.

"The stinkiest . . ." Antony continued.

"It was a good idea," I tried to argue.

But my brothers didn't think so. They moaned and groaned and whined and complained until I was getting a headache. They just didn't appreciate my good ideas. I thought the washing-powder looked really pretty. Just like real snow!

The Biggest Snowball In The Universe

When I woke up, my bedroom was really bright, even though the curtains were mostly drawn.

"Oh no! It's sunny," I said to myself.

If it was sunny then it would be too warm for snow. I walked slowly to the curtains and drew them back and there was . . . SNOW! The grass, our apple tree, the garden shed, they were all covered in lots and lots of snow. Inches and INCHES of snow.

Yippee!

I quickly had my wash and rushed downstairs.

"Mum, Mum! There's snow in our garden."

"Yes, I know," Mum said glumly. 'I left my clothes hanging out last night and now they're frozen stiff. I'm going to have to let them thaw out and wash them all over again."

"Maxine, it's been snowing." My brothers came running into the kitchen, and started hopping up and down as they looked out of the kitchen window at our garden.

"What are we going to do? Build a snow-castle?" I asked.

Snow-castles are the winter version of sand-castles.

"Build a snowman?" asked Antony.

"Have a snowball fight?" said Edward.

"You're all going to have some breakfast before you do anything else," Mum interrupted.

"Then can we go to the park, Mum? Please, please!" I begged.

"All right then. As long as you all stay out of trouble," Mum said.

So after breakfast, we set off for the park. There was a group of carol singers singing near the children's playground and a few people building snowmen and having snowball fights.

"Mum, can we climb up the hill?" I asked.

"Why?" Mum frowned.

"Then we can see everyone in the park," said Antony.

"Then we can see for miles and miles," added Edward.

"Well I'm not climbing up there," Mum replied, "I'll sit on a bench and watch you – AND DON'T GET INTO TROUBLE."

"Of course we won't get into trouble," I said, crossing my fingers behind my back.

We don't go looking for trouble, it just seems to sneak up behind us!

We climbed up the hilly bit of the park and we could see all the houses for miles around. It was ace-blazing! Double ace-blazing!

"What shall we do?" I asked.

"Let's do something special," said Antony.

"Something mega-ace special," agreed Edward.

"Hhmm!" I said. "I think this is a job for Girl Wonder and . . ."

"The Terrific Twins!" Antony and Edward called out.

And we all spun around until we were wobbly woozy and slipping and sliding all over the place.

"I know," I said. "Let's build a snowball. The hugest snowball in the world. And we can leave it here, at the top of the hill for everyone to see who comes to the park. They'll all look at it and say 'Isn't that the most ace-blazing snowball?'"

"Yeah, let's do that," Antony said.

"Right this second!" said Edward.

So we started building our snowball. At first it was the size of a marble; then the size of an orange; then the size of a football;

then the size of the globe at school – and it got bigger and Bigger and BIGGER.

"This is fun," Antony laughed.

"This snowball is going to be the biggest and best in the world," said Edward.

"The galaxy," Antony said.

"The universe," I argued.

And the snowball got bigger and bigger until it was almost as high as my brothers' waists and still we kept piling more snow on it.

Now it was as high as the twins' chests.

"We've done it," I said proudly. "We've built the biggest snowball in the universe."

"Let's make it even bigger," said Antony. "There's plenty of snow around."

"Yeah, don't stop yet," Edward pleaded.

"OK then," I replied, and we trotted a bit down the hill to get more fresh snow.

We were walking up the hill with our arms full of snow when I saw that our snowball was rocking backwards and forwards.

"Look, look!" We all started laughing.

But then the snowball took one great rock backwards, then one giant rock forwards and started to roll off down the hill.

"Oh no!" I shouted. "Quick, Terrific Twins, we have to stop it."

We dropped the snow in our hands and started running after our runaway snowball.

"Oh no!" I said, huffing and puffing as

we ran down the hill. Our runaway snowball was growing bigger and bigger as it
rolled – and it was heading straight for the
carol singers.

"Look out below!" I shouted.

"Watch out!" Antony called.

"It's coming! It's coming," Edward
yelled.

"MAXINE . . . EDWARD . . .
ANTONY . . . !" I heard Mum calling us
but we couldn't stop.

And still the runaway snowball kept growing as it collected more snow rolling down the hill. We were still running after the snowball trying to catch up with it. At last the carol singers heard us. They stopped singing and stared up the hill.

"Look out!" we bellowed.

The singers dived out of the way. There were legs and arms everywhere. Our ginormous, runaway snowball hit the railings around the children's playground and collapsed.

The carol singers stood up, dusting the snow off their clothes and glaring at us.

Ooops!

"Maxine, Antony, Edward, what did I say about staying out of trouble?" Mum asked, her hands on her hips.

"But Mum, it wasn't our fault. The snowball ran away from us," I said.

"I don't want to hear another word," Mum said. "We're going home. Right this minute. Right this moment."

"This is all your fault," Antony whispered, as we walked back home. "It was your idea."

"It was a good idea," I argued.

"It was a flimsy-floppy idea," pouted Antony.

"A seriously flimsy-floppy idea," sulked Edward.

"But at least it worked," I said. "We did build the biggest snowball in the universe."

Jayne,
The Pain!

It was going to be a rotten day. We had to go and see Aunt Joanne and Uncle Stan and worst of all our cousin Jayne.

My brothers and I made up a rhyme about our cousin.

> *Cousin Jayne*
> *Is a pain.*
> *If she's naughty,*
> *We're to blame!*

We're not too keen on our cousin. She gets on our nerves. She's always showing off about her new dress, or new hat, or new bike or new something or other. Every time we go to her house she's always got something new. And she never shares anything.

She's so wet!

Mum drove us to Aunt Joanne and Uncle Stan's house because it was too cold to walk through the park (which was how we usually got there).

"Maxine, Edward, Antony, I want you three on your very best behaviour," Mum said just before we got out of the car. "Every time we come here, you three seem to look for trouble to get into."

We don't look for trouble – it just seems to find us!

Mum got out of the car and walked up the garden path. We dawdled behind her. I walked up the garden path last. I think I'd rather go to the dentist than see my cousin Jayne.

"Hello everyone." Aunt Joanne opened the door before Mum even rang the door bell.

"My goodness, Maxine, haven't you grown!" Auntie bent down and kissed me on the cheek. She always says that. She always does that. And I hate it!

Yuk! In fact, double yuk!

"Hello, Maxine, Hi, Ed and Tony," Drippy Jayne said to us. "Come and see my new toboggan."

I looked at the twins. They looked at me. It hadn't taken her long to show off this time. It must have been all of about five seconds!

"What's a toboggan?" Antony asked.

"Yeah, what's that?" Edward added.

"It's like a sledge that I can lie on or sit on. Then I can slide over the snow," Jayne said with her nose in the air. "I can go really fast. It's a really good toboggan."

"Go on you three," Mum said. "Go into the garden and have a look at Jayne's toboggan."

We dragged our feet and walked slowly as we followed Jayne out into the garden. I

did want to see the toboggan but I didn't want to see Jayne show off.

"Isn't it terrific?" Jayne said, dusting some snow off it.

I must admit it did look good, and Jayne's garden was just perfect for tobogganing. It was huge and ever so slightly hilly, so that there was enough of a slope for the toboggan to whizz along but not too much of a mountain for the toboggan to get out of control. I was longing to try it out but I knew it was no use asking Jayne. She liked to show us all her new things but she never let us touch any of them.

"Watch me,' Jayne ordered, going to the far end of her enormous garden. As we watched, she lay down on her toboggan and kicked off with her feet.

WH-III-SH!

Jayne came skiing down the slope. She dug her toes into the snow to stop the toboggan just before it got to us.

"Watch me again," she commanded, running back up the garden.

"Maxine, can't we have a go?" Antony whispered to me.

"Maxine, I want a go on the toboggan," Edward said.

"It's up to Jayne, not me." I shrugged.

"Huh! Then we might as well go indoors," Antony sighed.

"Right this second!" Edward agreed.

"Don't give up yet. We're each going to have a go on Jayne's toboggan before leaving for home," I said.

"How?" asked Antony.

"Do you have a plan?" asked Edward.

"Not yet but maybe this is a job for Girl Wonder . . ."

"And the Terrific Twins," my brothers said without much enthusiasm, and we spun around slowly so that we didn't skate

57

and glide and slip and slide over the snow.

"Here I come!" shouted Jayne from the other end of the garden.

SHH-WHISH!

Jayne whooshed over the snow, stopping just in front of us again.

"Watch me again," she demanded. She ran back up the garden, dragging her toboggan behind her.

"Pretend you're not really interested in what she's doing," I whispered to the Terrific Twins as Jayne tobogganed towards us.

"Come on you two, let's make a snowman," I said out loud.

We moved out of Jayne's way and knelt down. Then we started piling up snow to make the snowman's body.

"Don't you want to watch me?" Jayne asked, puzzled.

"Why should we?" I replied. "We're building a snowman."

"A big snowman," said Antony.

"A huge snowman," said Edward.

"The best snowman in the world," I told Jayne.

And we piled up more snow. Jayne stood watching us for a while, her toboggan behind her.

"Why don't you want to watch me?" Jayne asked, even more puzzled.

"We did watch you. Now we're doing something else," I replied.

"Something far more exciting," added Antony.

"Something much, much more interesting," said Edward.

Then cousin Jayne, the pain, did something really nasty. She walked over to us and kicked our snowman's body over. The Terrific Twins and I jumped to our feet.

"You rotten, spiteful cat," yelled
Antony.

"You nasty, mean toad," shouted
Edward.

"Is it any wonder we don't like you?" I told Jayne. I was furious. "Whenever we see you all you do is show off and boast about what you've got and you never share anything. You're selfish and spoilt and we hate coming to your house. We mega-hate it. I bet you've got no friends at school. I bet no one likes you."

The Terrific Twins and I glared at her. Jayne glared back but her bottom lip was trembling. Then her face scrunched up and she burst into tears.

"Would anyone like a hot drink?" Uncle Stan asked from the kitchen doorway before he saw Jayne crying. "Maxine, Antony, Edward, what have you been doing to Jayne?"

Uncle Stan looked really annoyed with us.

On either side of him stood Aunt Joanne and our mum, looking really stern.

"We didn't do anything, Mum . . ." I said quickly.

"No, we didn't," said Antony.

"Not a thing," said Edward.

"Jayne dear, did they hurt you?" Aunt Joanne came out into the garden in her slippers and hugged Jayne.

'Maxine, why is Jayne crying?" Mum asked quietly.

I looked at the twins, they looked at me. None of us said a word.

"It . . . it wasn't them," Jayne whispered to her mum. "I . . . I fell off my toboggan."

I stared at her. She was taking the blame!

"Are you hurt, my precious?" Aunt Joanne asked Jayne.

"No, I'm fine," Jayne sniffed before wiping her eyes. "Maxine and Antony and Edward are going to use my toboggan and I'm going to help them build a snowman."

"Maxine, are you all OK?" Mum asked.

"Yes, Mum," the twins and I said.

"Well, don't stay out too long," Mum said.

"We won't," we replied.

"Come on, Joanne, before you catch a cold," Mum said to our aunt.

The grown-ups walked back into the kitchen and shut the kitchen door behind them. My brothers and I looked at Jayne.

"Did you mean it about letting us use your toboggan?" I asked suspiciously.

"Only if you let me help you with your snowman," Jayne replied.

"It's a deal," I said.

The twins and I had great fun tobogganing down Jayne's garden. Each of us kept falling off until Jayne told us how to do it properly. It was just as well that the snow was soft. After that we built a huge snowman. Jayne got us a carrot to use as the nose and two satsumas to use as the eyes and she wasn't a pain at all. Our snowman was the best in the world. We had the most fun we'd ever had at Jayne's house.

We didn't mean to make her cry but at least our plan worked – sort of. We did all get to use Jayne's toboggan.

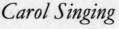

Carol Singing

"Mum, everyone in my class is doing something to collect money for charity," I said when I came home from school. "I thought that maybe the twins and I could go carol singing and we could collect money that way. Will you take us? Please, *please*."

"Carol singing. Hooray!" said Antony.

"Yahzoo! Carol singing," said Edward.

Mum frowned. 'Oh all right. We'll go tonight – but only tonight."

"Thanks, Mum," we said.

"Come on you two. We're going to practise," I said to my brothers.

We ran upstairs and into Edward's and

67

Antony's bedroom, shutting the door behind us.

"Edward, Antony, we're going to collect a lot of money for charity," I said. "And we're going to be the most ace-dazzling carol singers ever."

"We are?" asked Antony.

"Are we?" asked Edward.

"Yes we are," I said firmly. "And just to make sure I think this is a job for Girl Wonder . . ."

"And the Terrific Twins," said my brothers. And we spun around until we rolled and reeled all over the place.

We practised and practised until we could remember the words of each of the four songs we were going to sing – 'Silent Night', 'Oh Come, All Ye Faithful', 'We Wish You a Merry Christmas' and 'Every Star Shall Sing a Carol'. We couldn't wait for evening to arrive.

At last it was time to set off. We had my drum and Antony's red trumpet. We all

went to Miss Ree's house first.

Antony played his trumpet –
ROOOOMPH! ROOOOMPH! and I
banged my drum – DUUUM! DUUUM!
– and Edward and I started singing.

"We wish you a merry christmas . . ."

"Good grief! What is that ghastly
racket?" Miss Ree said after pulling open
her front door. "Maxine, Antony, Edward,
what are you three doing?"

I turned around to look at Mum. She was at Miss Ree's gate and looking any-where except at us.

"We're carol singing, Miss Ree," I re-plied. 'If you want to donate something we're collecting for charity."

"Will you go away if I give you some money?" Miss Ree asked.

"Yes." I frowned.

Miss Ree dug into her skirt pocket, gave us a coin and quickly shut the door.

"I don't think she liked our singing . . ." Antony said.

"Maybe she didn't like the song," said Edward.

"She's just a misery and doesn't have

any taste," I decided. "It's a shame though. We didn't even get past the first line of 'We Wish You a Merry Christmas'."

"But we're doing really well," said Antony. "We've already collected some money for charity."

"This is fun," added Edward.

"Let's try Mr McBain," I suggested.

Mr McBain is our other next door neighbour. We walked up to his front door.

Antony blew his trumpet – ROOOOMPH! ROOOOMPH! – I banged my drum – DUUUM! DUUUM! – and we started singing.

"Oh come, all ye faithful . . ."

Mr McBain opened his door.

"What is that dreadful din?" he said.

"We're collecting for charity, Mr McBain," Edward said.

Mr McBain dug into his trouser pockets.

"Here, take that," he said, handing us five coins. "It's all I've got but take it, *please*."

And he shut the door.

"Hhmm!" I said. "He doesn't appreciate
good singing either."

We went to the next house.

"Silent night, holy night . . ." we sang.

The front door was flung open.

"What a frightful noise," Mrs Johnson said.

When she saw us she took some coins out of the drawer of the little table in her hall. She didn't even wait for us to explain that we were collecting for charity!

When she closed the door we looked around for Mum. She appeared from behind Mr and Mrs Johnson's car.

"You were hiding, Mum!" I said.

"Er . . . no I wasn't," Mum replied. "My shoe slipped off and I just went back for it."

"I think Mum was hiding," Antony whispered to me.

"I *know* Mum was hiding," Edward said.

We went to three more houses. At each house we didn't even finish the first two lines of our carols before we were paid by our neighbours to go away.

"That's it," Mum said, her eyes glinting. "I can't take any more embarrassment. I'll never be able to look our neighbours in the eye again. We're all going home – NOW!"

"But Mum, we're collecting for charity," we argued.

"No 'buts'," Mum said. "As it's for a good cause I'll sponsor all three of you when we get home."

"Sponsored carol singing?" I asked.

"No, a sponsored silence!" Mum replied.

"Our singing isn't that bad," mumbled Antony.

"Yeah, it can't be that bad," Edward grumbled.

"It's WORSE!" Mum replied. "You three have given me a raging headache!"

We all walked home. I thought we'd been quite good!

"That didn't work out very well," Antony said.

"That didn't work out very well at all," agreed Edward sadly.

"But it sort of worked," I whispered. "We are going to raise some money for charity through our carol singing."

"Mum's paying us NOT to sing," said the twins.

"Exactly!" I replied.

Christmas
Spying And
Prying

We were bursting to know what Mum had bought us for Christmas but she wouldn't tell us.

"Did you buy me a space cavalier outfit?" I asked. "And did you get the science kit belt that goes with it? I've got to have the science kit belt. Then I can test for new plants and animals on other planets."

"What about my model plane kit? Mum, is that what you bought me? Is it? Is it?" Antony asked, jumping up and down.

"Did you get me a toy guitar? Please, *please* say yes," said Edward. Mum just smiled and said nothing.

When the twins went out into the garden to throw snowballs at each other, I tugged at Mum's arm.

"What did you get us for Christmas? I'll keep it a secret. I won't tell the twins — honest," I whispered to Mum.

"If I don't tell you then you won't have any secrets inside you bursting to get out,' Mum replied. "I know you, Maxine, you can't keep a secret to save your life."

"I can, I can," I said.

"No you can't. If I told you, the secret would sit inside your chest like a balloon. And the more you tried to say nothing, the more that balloon would grow. It would get bigger and Bigger and BIGGER until it EXPLODED from you!"

"Hhmm!" I sulked. I got the feeling Mum wasn't going to tell me, no matter how much I begged.

I put on my coat and my wellies and stomped out into the garden. CRUNCH! CRUNCH! went the snow under my feet.

It was just like walking on scrunched, crunched, crushed, crumbled ginger biscuits.

"Did you find out what we're getting for Christmas?" asked Antony.

"Yeah, did you?" Edward said.

"No . . . but I've got a plan," I said.

79

"This is a job for Girl Wonder . . ."

"And the Terrific Twins," Antony and Edward shouted. "Hooray!" And we spun around until we fell down, whirling-swirling dizzy.

"It's a really good plan," I said. "Tonight when Mum's asleep, we'll sneak downstairs and open our presents at just one end. Then we'll be able to see what Mum bought us without Mum ever finding out about it."

"If Mum catches us we'll be in serious trouble." Antony frowned.

"Yeah, seriously serious trouble," agreed Edward.

"Then we won't wake her up," I said.

"This had better work, Maxine," Antony told me, his arms folded across his chest. "If we get caught then I'm blaming you."

"Of course it'll work," I said, crossing all my fingers and even crossing my toes.

That night I had to fight to stay awake. Mum stayed up watching the telly for ages and ages. My eyes felt so sandy and sleepy that I had to keep pinching myself to stay awake. At last I heard Mum come up the stairs and go to bed. I searched for Mum's torch under my pillow. (I'd hidden it there when I came to bed.) I switched on the torch and pointed it down at the carpet – I didn't want to trip over my slippers and wake up Mum. I got up carefully and tip-toed out of my bedroom and into the twins' bedroom. They were fast asleep in their bunk beds.

"Wake up," I hissed at them, giving them a good shake. "Wake up, it's Girl Wonder . . ."

"And the sleepy Terrific Twins . . ." Antony said drowsily, before turning over and going back to sleep.

"Come on you two," I whispered. "Don't you want to know what Mum's bought us for Christmas?"

They moaned and grumbled, grumbled and moaned but at last I managed to get them out of their beds. I led the way downstairs, shining the torch as the three of us crept down the outside of the stairs. We had to creep down the outside because the middle of each stair creaks horribly. We tip-toed over to our presents scattered underneath the Christmas tree. The twins were fully awake now.

About time too! I thought.

We knelt down and searched for our

presents from Mum. It was exciting. Antony found his present first.

"Open it carefully," I whispered. "We don't want Mum to know that we had a peek."

Slowly Antony peeled back the sticky tape on one side of his present. Carefully he pulled it out from the wrapping paper. It was a book. I shone my torch on it. *Maths For Everyone* it said on the front.

"Yuk!" Antony wailed. "Where's my model plane kit?"

"Shush! Or Mum will catch us," I whispered.

Edward opened his present next. It was another book. *English For Everyone*.

"Double yuk!" wailed Edward. "Where's my toy guitar?"

Next I opened my present. It was the same size as Antony and Edward's so I didn't hold out much hope.

Science For Everyone.

"What happened to my space cavalier's outfit?" I said sadly.

"I wish you'd never woken us up now," Antony said to me.

"Yeah, me too," Edward said.

We all walked slowly up the stairs and the twins went into their bedroom whilst I went back into mine. I was so looking forward to my space cavalier's suit. A science book wasn't the same at all.

The next morning, it was CHRIST-MAS DAY. It might as well have been a school day! The twins and I didn't say much as we ate our Christmas breakfast, listening to the hymns on the telly.

"What's the matter with you three?" Mum smiled. She had a really funny look on her face, as if she was trying her best not to burst out laughing.

"Nothing . . ." Antony sighed.

"Nothing . . ." Edward sighed even harder.

"Nothing . . ." I put my head on my hands.

"Aren't any of you going to open your

presents?" Mum asked. "I thought you would do that before anything else this morning."

"There's no point . . ." Antony began before I kicked him under the table.

"Why is there no point?" Mum asked, her hands on her hips. "Do you already know what your presents are? I hope you three haven't been getting up in the middle of the night to see what I bought you . . ."

The twins and I looked at each other guiltily.

"Of course not, Mum," I said quickly.

"Hhmm!" Mum replied. "Well, if you don't open your presents soon I'm going to think that you don't want them."

We got up and went over to the Christmas tree.

"That's your present," Mum said, handing a present to Edward – a present that was guitar-shaped.

Edward tore off the paper. It was a guitar. A brown guitar with red strings.

"Hooray!" Edward shouted.

"And this is yours," Mum said, handing Antony his present.

Antony tore off the wrapping paper. It was a model plane kit. It was just what Antony wanted. The one where you had to glue all the pieces together yourself and then paint them.

"Yippee!" Antony clapped his hands.

"Your turn, Maxine," Mum said,

handing me a large, square-shaped present. It was too big to be the smelly *Science For Everyone* book. I ripped off the paper.

It was my space cavalier outfit with a special science kit belt for finding new animal and plant life on other planets.

"Thanks, Mum." We all grinned. "Thanks very much."

"But what happened to the books?" Antony asked.

"What books?" Mum frowned.

"The books that were under the Christmas tree last night," Edward said before I could stop him.

I could have kicked him!

"I think you two must have been dreaming," Mum said sternly. "I know my children wouldn't be so sneaky as to try to open their presents before Christmas Day, unless they were dreaming about opening them. Isn't that right, Maxine?"

"Yes!" I agreed, quickly. "Merry Christmas, Mum."

"Yeah, Happy Christmas," said Edward.

"It's Christmas, Mum," said Antony.

"Merry Christmas, to us all," said Mum. And we all hugged each other, tight, tight, tight.

Then Mum walked back into the kitchen – and she was smiling.

Hank Prank
and
Hot Henrietta

Jules Older

**You'll never meet a pair *quite* like
Hank Prank and Hot Henrietta!**

What can you do with an impossible duo
like Hank Prank and Hot Henrietta?
Well, their parents and teachers do try
their best to keep them under control –
but not always with much success!

Also in Young Puffin

Mrs Pepperpot

in the Magic Wood

Alf Prøysen

Nine delightfully funny stories about that incredible shrinking woman, Mrs Pepperpot!

How would *you* feel if you suddenly shrank to the size of a pepperpot? Well, that's exactly what happens to Mrs Pepperpot – and always at the most awkward moments. But it *does* lead her into a lot of very exciting adventures in which she meets some very unusual characters!